Postman Pat's
Thirsty Day

Story by **John Cunliffe** *Pictures by* **Celia Berridge**

from the original Television designs by **Ivor Wood**

ANDRE DEUTSCH

First published 1984 by
André Deutsch Limited
105 Great Russell Street London WC1B 3LJ

Phototypeset by Diagraphic Limited
Printed in Great Britain by Cambus Litho, East Kilbride, Scotland

ISBN 0 233 97675 2

It was another hot day in Greendale...a *very* hot day.
In the fields, the sheep looked for any patch of shade – under a tree, behind a wall.
They gathered there, panting, in their woolly coats.

"It's a real scorcher to-day," said Pat to Jess, as they drove along. "Phew, I'm thirsty already."

The lakes were drying up. The stream was down to a trickle.

At the village post-office, Mrs. Goggins was outside, looking out for Pat, and trying to get cool.

"Morning Pat!" she called. "Isn't it hot! *And* we're going to be without water to-day."

"I know," said Pat, "the lake's really low and they're going to turn the water off this morning. Whatever will we do?"

"Well, I've filled the kettle and two pans," said Mrs. Goggins.

They went into the post-office. Mrs. Goggins took a bottle of lemonade out of the fridge. She said, "But they can't turn the lemonade off. There you are, Pat, have a drink before you go."

"Mmmmm...lovely," said Pat, "thank you, just what I need...My, that's good...that's much better. Well, I'd better be on my way. Thanks for the drink! Cheerio!"

Pat collected his letters and parcels. There was a parcel marked FRAGILE, for Granny Dryden.

"Now take good care of that," said Mrs. Goggins. "It looks like something from that catalogue of hers."

"I will," said Pat. "I ordered a watch from her. It might be that. Cheerio!"

Pat was on his way.

He began his round with the village letters. Along the winding streets, through narrow passageways, in and out of cottage gardens he went, and everyone was pleased to see him.

He met Granny Dryden out shopping, and told her about the parcel. "It's in the van," he said. "I'll pop in with it later." Then he told her about the water being cut off.

"Well, it's a pity the old pump isn't working," she said. "There were plenty of dry summers in my young days, and, do you know, that pump *never* dried up, not once!"

"I wonder," said Pat. "I wonder if Ted Glen could mend it? I must ask him. He can fix just about anything."

Pat tried the rusty handle of the pump, as he passed it, but it wouldn't move. He finished the village letters, then set out for the farms in his van.

At Greendale Farm, the water was already off. Peter Fogg was winding buckets of water up from the old well, to get water for the cows. Katy and Tom were helping to carry the water to the trough.

"Hello," said Pat. "You still have water in the well, then? Let's have a look."
He bent over to peer into the mossy depths. He could hear water splashing and
dripping, but it was too dark and deep to see. He bent further, then – "Ooooops!"
– his hat slipped off and dropped into the well.

"Oh dear," said Pat, "I'll never see that again."

"I wonder if I can fish it out with the hook," said Peter. "Let's try."

He lowered the hook without the bucket on it, and swung it about at the bottom. When he wound it up again, Pat's hat was on it, dripping wet, and trailing strands of water-weed.

"It will be nice and cool, anyway," said Peter.

"Thanks," said Pat. "Now I mustn't drop your letters down the well."

"No," said Peter. "Thanks, Pat – and would you mind dropping off a drum of water for George Lancaster? He hasn't got a well, or a spring, so he must be desperate for water by now."

"Certainly," said Pat. "We'll be going past his road-end. Cheerio!"

High in the hills, at Intake Farm, George Lancaster had no water at all. He was very glad to see the big plastic drum of water in the back of Pat's van.

"Special delivery," said Pat. "A parcel of water. There's no address on it, but it looks pretty dry here, so I think it must be for you."

"Thanks, Pat," said George. "You've saved my life. We've dried out completely up here."

Pat remembered to call at Ted Glen's workshop to ask if Ted could mend the old
village pump.

"Well, I don't know," said Ted, "That pump hasn't been used since I was a
boy. The works may be all rusted away. But Granny Dryden's lived all her life in
Greendale, and she knows a thing or two, so she could be right about that pump.
Besides, my water's been off all morning, and I'm thirsty, so it's worth a try. I'll
just get my tools. Leave it to me!"

At Thompson Ground, Dorothy Thompson was enjoying a cup of tea, when Pat called with a letter.

"Hello," said Pat, "isn't your water off? Everyone else's is."

"No, we have a spring," said Mrs. Thompson. "It comes out of the hillside just above the house. It's never been known to dry up – not since grandad was a boy, anyway, and that was a very long time ago."

"You *are* lucky," said Pat, and he told her about the village pump. "I wonder how Ted's getting on?"

Down in the village, Ted was very busy. He was hard at work on that old pump, and a crowd had gathered to watch and cheer him on. Mrs. Goggins brought him a pot of tea to keep him going.

Miss Hubbard brought him a frying-pan that needed mending. The Reverend Timms promised to say a prayer for rain, at Evensong. Alf Thompson said there was nothing like a really good spring. But Ted just kept on working.

He carefully took everything to pieces. He put oil and grease on the rusty
bearings, and cleaned all the rust away. He hammered a bent rod until it was
ruler-straight. He fitted a new washer. He cleaned fifty years of rubbish out of the
pipes – old twigs and leaves, newspapers, dirty rags, a dead mouse. At last, he put
the pump together again. He tightened everything up, and screwed the top on.

"Now then; let's see," he said. He worked the handle up and down. Nothing happened. "It's gone dry," someone said. He tried again.

There was a gurgle deep in the pipes. Again. A spurt of rusty water gushed out, wetting everyone! "Hurrah!" they all cheered.

Ted went on pumping. The water ran rusty-golden for a time, then it came clean and clear. Pat arrived in time to see it.

"I knew you'd do it," he said. "I just knew you would. Granny Dryden *will* be pleased. I'll take her some water, to celebrate."

Everyone queued up to fill their cans and buckets, and thank Ted. Jess came for a drink, and had an unexpected shower.

When Pat called on Granny Dryden, he told her all about how Ted had mended the pump, and gave her a can of water with her parcel. She was delighted.

"I'll have to come and see for myself," she said.

She opened the parcel. It was the new digital-watch that Pat had ordered from her catalogue.

"That's good," said Pat. "I'll always be on time, now. I'll bring the money to-morrow. Cheerio! Look after yourself!"

Pat had kept a can of water for himself. Jess kept a sharp eye on it, all the way home. He didn't want another wetting, no matter *how* hot it was.